This igloo book belongs

D0476338

....

igloobooks

Published in 2016
by Igloo Books Ltd
Cottage Farm
Sywell
NN6 0BJ
www.igloobooks.com

LEO002 0616
2 4 6 8 10 9 7 5 3
ISBN 978-1-78440-732-2

Written by Melanie Joyce
Illustrated by Gabrielle Murphy

Printed and manufactured in China

Love makes the world go round

igloobooks

Love is cuddling up when it's icy and cold.

Love is being tickled and tumbled and rolled.

Love is being lost and finding each other.

Love is my mum, dad, sister and brother.

Love is the best present you've ever had.

Love is a kiss when you are feeling so sad.

Love is happiness. It's giving and sharing.

Love is tenderness, kindness and caring.

Love makes the world go round and brings us together.

Love is about friendships that last forever.